Let's Talk About *THAT!*

By

Uma Kriko

Dedication

To my prodigy, Marton, the best teacher I could ever wish for. You are shining brighter than Venus in the velvety sky.

To my golden-hearted and noble Zsombor, whose love is pure and sincere. You are my full moon, who always shows the way out from the darkest night.

To my love Gyuri, who is always there for me even when I am not there for myself.

To my mom, who sacrificed so much so I could study, I am thankful to you.

To my paternal grandparents Papo and Mama, and also Danny, Luke, and Sara in heaven. They taught me the importance of the present moment and love with all my might because tomorrow is not promised to anyone.

To Amy and Dianna for your ongoing support

About the Book

This book was written based on radical honesty in parenting.

Answer questions considering the kid's current stage of development and understanding.

"So, every time you have intercourse, you will have a baby?"

Well, the moment the question was out, Uma realized there are two kinds of sex talk, the recreational and the other, that don't involve reproduction.

Radical honesty can be uncomfortable sometimes. There will always be questions that are hard to answer.

However, the world has changed so much. Excess to the internet lets young children seek answers, but unfortunately, they don't necessarily look in the right place.

Many children have no privilege to ask their parents because it's considered to be a taboo, surrounded by hazy guilt.

Some kids lost their parents and walked in the dark.

The author wants to provide a neutral opportunity for kids to fulfill their thirst for knowledge about topics of taboos such as sex and death.

Unfortunately, bullying became a norm. Our society

accepted it. Ill-minded people project their insecurity and point fingers, blaming others for their failures. So much injustice, and we close our eyes, pretend to be blind, or simply turn away. Adults insult minors, and men harass women. Women accuse men.

The book will discuss racism and bullying as well and will show a healthy way to cope with it.

Contents

Chapter One

Big Brother

Simon was an amusing, quick-witted, inquisitive, remarkable kid. He loved art and painted a beautiful picture for his soon-to-be-born brother daily. Yes, his mother Uma was expecting. She was round and chubby, like a full moon on a velvety midnight sky.

Simon had difficulty relaxing or falling asleep because his mind was always working; he always had so many questions. His mother answered all his questions tirelessly, ensuring her son had all the valid information from her, so he won't get scared if he heard something in school later.

Simon's aunt didn't think his mother Uma's radical honesty was the way of raising a kid, but aunty Gerthrud never had a child, so how would she know what's best for a kid? Simon and Uma had an unbelievably strong bond. They could talk about anything, and there was a deep mutual trust. They secretly called this trust the invisible golden rope, which nothing can destroy; that was their superpower.

One day, in early autumn, the canopies turned from green to dark orange and deep red; mama Uma and Papi told

Simon that he would have a sibling. Simon immediately started to flood them with questions. The 'how', the 'what', and the 'where' were hard to answer.

"Wow, mom, I am so excited! Will I have a brother or sister?" asked the clever little boy.

"We do not know yet, but next time at my checkup with my OB-GYN, we can ask if you want to know the gender."

Uma pulled out a picture from her purse and showed it to Simon.

"What is this?" Simon questioned.

"Well, this is an image of your sibling, just like photography. Only they take it with an ultrasound machine," Uma answered.

"What! How? The baby is in your belly! How can they take a photo of it? Does your doctor cut your belly so she can take a photo?"

"No, silly goose, she does not! The doctor uses a small tool on the mommy's belly. Then she applies some warm gel and moves the tool around to have the image of the baby."

"A tool?"

"Yes, a small ultrasound probe device is used, which gives off high-frequency sound waves. You can't hear these sound waves, but when they bounce off different body parts, they create 'echoes 'that are picked up by the probe and turned into a moving image. Next time, you can come with us and see it yourself."

"I definitely would love that mom, and I think I really want to know if it's a boy or girl so that we can choose a name!"

"Alright then! We will do so. Also, I will allow you to ask some questions from my OBGYN."

Simon started to giggle.

"Obi-Wan Kenobi is the name of your doctor? That's so silly!"

"Her name is not Obi-Wan Kenobi. It's an obstetrician, shortened OBGYN, who specializes in delivering babies and taking care of expecting mommies."

Simon was satisfied with the answers for a while. He decided to finish his daily chores. He walked his dog Cosmo, an adorable miniature dachshund. He also watered the plants he had planted for his science project two weeks before. Simon had chosen to plant six French marigolds from seeds and water them with different kinds of water – filtered, distilled, chlorine, tap, sparkling and alkaline. He had to observe, follow and write the difference between their four growth charts. Every other condition was the same; soil and temperature and the daily sunlight besides the water quality. His parents loved his project and were also keen to see the outcome.

Simon was tired and couldn't wait for supper. His favorite meal was dinner because they all sat at the table talking.

His mother cooked every night, but lately, his father substituted for her, because Uma was often tired or nauseated. She was bothered by the strong smell, and she often complained about those annoying hormones. She also was really emotional, so Papi taught Simon how to read the room and let mama Uma have some space.

"Reading the room means being aware of people's feelings when you enter a room and interact with anyone," Papi explained to Simon. "You see, mom is tired. Look at her posture. She holds her back and sighs with teary eyes. So, I let her sit and massage her feet before dinner so she can feel better."

Simon nodded. He wanted to contribute to his mother's relaxation, so he filled a glass of chilled hibiscus-mint tea and served it to her. Uma was grateful to them and felt better immediately.

"Mom, what are those crazy hormones you are talking about? Is it something that makes you sick? Why are you throwing up so much?"

"Hormones are your body's chemical messengers. They travel in your bloodstream to tissues or organs. They work slowly over time and affect many processes, including growth and development. Metabolism is when your body gets energy from the foods you eat, then sexual function, reproduction, and mood. Many different hormones are responsible for a pregnant lady to be nauseated and sick."

"Everybody throws up during pregnancy?"

"No, absolutely not, but some do, just like me."

"Does it hurt?"

"No, it doesn't hurt, but definitely uncomfortable."

"Oh, I am sorry you are one of those mommies. I don't like to throw up. Were you sick when you expected me?"

"Yep, I was. Mommy had a little challenge, but it is worth every second because I have wanted to have you since I became a young woman. You are everything I imagined. A baby is a blessing when you wish to have one."

"Mom! But how does it get in your belly? Is it in your stomach?"

"In my womb! The womb is separated from the stomach. Look, the stomach is up here, and the womb is set lower."

'So? Mom? How did it get there? I heard the 6th graders saying that when parents are sexing, they make a baby."

'Sexing?" asked Uma.

"Yes, something like that. They saw it on the internet, and Jefferson said it's when parents kiss and get naked and hide under the blanket that 's when they make a baby."

Uma realized she was right to choose radical honesty in her parenting because she never wanted her kids to be confused or have the wrong information, nor to have a bitter, ill perception about reproduction or love.

"Well, let's have your shower, and we can continue this conversation, darling," said his mother in a chuckling voice.

"Mom, what is so funny?"

"You are! One of the funniest little boy, Simon!

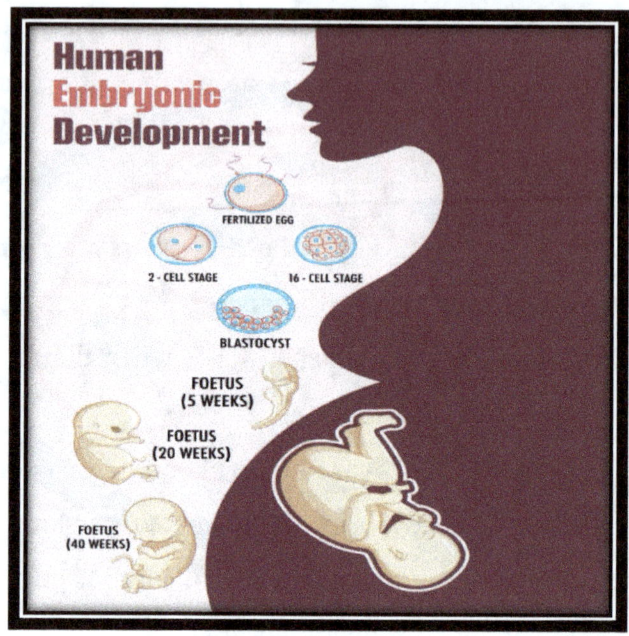

The shower went quickly, and the sun was ready to set. The family watched the sunset together from the lanai, waiting for the full moon to rise. This was one of Uma's favorite monthly magical events. Simon also loved to watch the moon rise. He thought it was mesmerizing. He got lost in the starry sky as he studied the constellations with his new telescope. They were fortunate to have a house on the shore.

"Heaven is for real if you live by the ocean," sighed Uma.

They all agreed that the sunset was mesmerizing and felt otherworldly. Before it set for the day, it covered everything with its warm pinkish, purplish, and orange rays.

After it entirely disappeared, the darkness crept upon them. The temperature dropped immediately. Lightning appeared in the dark blue, velvety sky and gently warned them about the coming storm.

They were ready for the moon to rise. While waiting for the very first sign of the moon to show off its silver rays, Uma was looking around, feeling grateful; for everything she had and everyone she met. Her heart filled with gratitude, watching the boys and the dog.

It was quiet and peaceful; there were no airplanes or cruise ships around, only a few sailboats far away on the horizon. On their far left, the evening lights of the nearby city sparkled like shiny rubies and diamonds. Hiding behind the evening fog, the waves trembled and strengthened. The tide was ready to show its power, trying to sweep away the man far on the shore. He tried so hard to resist the ocean, but it was bigger than life, so powerful, and pulled the sand under his feet. Simon giggled, watching the man battle with the waves.

Uma closed her eyes, listening to the ocean washing the shore. Its tremble synchronized with her heartbeat. The smell of the coming storm, the overwhelming smell of the dead seaweed, and the salty ocean satisfied her soul.

Their next-door neighbor started to burn Palo Santo

and play the drum. Mr. Peer-peer was very spiritual, and his chanting flew high in the breeze. It was peaceful. Uma opened her eyes just in time, watching the moon picking through the horizon. It was enormous!

First, it appeared fiery orange from the setting sun - the yin and the yang. Only for a second, they meet twice a day, reaching out for each other, joining for a nanosecond, just like platonic lovers, then fast departing again.

The sun left so the moon could shine independently, with all its potential being whole without the sun. They watched the moon rise higher and higher, playing peekaboo, hiding behind the fluffy dark clouds. Its silver rays were gently dancing on the deep blue ocean, showing the path back home for the fishermen.

It started to be late, and it was time to get ready to rest. Simon was uneased at night; he never liked the evenings. Today, however, he was thrilled to know that soon he won't be an only child. Soon he will have a roommate - a tiny baby, who will probably cry a lot, but he wouldn't mind. After all, the little munchkin would be his baby brother!

Chapter Two

Are You Ready for The Truth

Instead of watching his show before bed, Simon chose to talk. He was impatient to find out the truth about the myth of baby-making. His mother's voice was comforting and solid.

"So, are you ready for the truth?"

"I think so," he replied.

"All right. I want you to know you can ask questions, and I can cease anytime you are uncomfortable."

"You are a funny mom. Have you ever seen me uncomfortable? Well, maybe when my great-grandpa Michael farted at the wedding!" They both blushed and laughed loudly.

"Oh yes, I remember that was very uncomfortable… so, you said you heard a few things already from the middle schoolers. You also said they might have the information from the internet. Hmm…you see…electronics can be a blessing and curse if you don't know how to use them properly," Uma explained. "Reproduction means to reproduce. It is a biological process that ensures the continuity of species, generation after generation. It is the main feature of life on earth. The male gamete, or sperm, and the female gamete, the ovum, meet in the female reproductive system. When sperm fertilizes (meets) the ovum, this fertilized ovum is called a zygote (ZYE-goat)."

Simon watched his mom explain without blinking, concentrating on every word she said.

"Each sperm is extremely small: only 1/600 of an inch (0.05 millimeters long)." Uma continued. "Sperm develop in the testicles within a system of tiny tubes called seminiferous tubules. Ovum, plural ova, in human physiology, single-cell released from either of the female reproductive organs, the ovaries, which can develop into a new organism when fertilized (united) with a sperm cell."

"Is it the women's egg?"

"The professional term is the ovum, but they call it egg as well."

"So how will that sperm get close to the ovum? How can they meet to make that ZEE goat?"

Uma laughed again and gently corrected Simon, saying, "It's not a Z- goat; it's a zygote. It is the beginning of a new human two cells union. They unite with intercourse. Intercourse is when the male genitalia, the men's penis, enters the female vagina."

"Enters?" asked the boy.

"Yes, when a man's penis gets hard, we call it an erection, and with a gentle push, he enters the woman's vagina. Through ejaculation, the sperm exits the testicles through the penis and unites with the ovum. Then, the sperm fuses with the ovum."

"How many sperm ejaculates at once?"

"Millions, but only one or two, sometimes even a little more, can fuse with an ovum. Women usually have one ripe ovum every month. Sometimes it could be more. That's when they can have twins or triplets. So, intercourse is sex. You told me the 6th graders referred to sexing, but it's sex. Do you understand so far?"

"I do. But you said the egg - the ovum has to be ripe? Like, a mango?"

"Well, it is a process we call menstruation, which means the female body is physically capable of becoming pregnant. In the first half of the menstrual cycle, levels of the hormone estrogen rise, making the lining of the uterus thicken. This lining nourishes a fertilized egg (embryo) if pregnancy occurs. A menstruation period is when blood comes through a girl's vagina. Menstrual flow is involuntary. Girls cannot stop it for 5 to 7 days every month. It is a sign that she is getting close to end of puberty. Puberty is when your body goes from looking like a kid to looking more like a grown-up."

"Oh, is this why I have seen dirty, bloody things in public restrooms?"

"Yes, those were pads or tampons that women used during their period. Those you saw weren't appropriately wrapped."

"When does a girl start to have ripe eggs?"

"The average is between 10 to 15 years old, but mommy got her first period at age eight and Grandma Greta at 17. Women are only fertile until menopause. Menopause is when a woman's hormone level decreases, lessens, and she won't produce more eggs or ovum, and they won't have a period."

He was quietly staring at the ceiling. Uma knew he was not satisfied with the answers yet. She needed to be patient so that he could process the information. "Do you understand so far?" Uma asked politely.

"So, every time you have intercourse, you will have a baby?"

Well, the moment the question was out, Uma realized there are two kinds of sex talk, the recreational one and the other that doesn't involve reproduction.

"No, you won't always have a baby when you have intercourse. When two people have feelings for each other, they can get intimate, which often involves sex."

'Oh. Ok. All right, I see. But... does sex hurt?"

'I can't talk for a man. You got to ask your father, but the first few intercourses for women could be uncomfortable. The entry of the vagina has a soft, thin piece of tissue called the hymen. When that gets broken by intercourse, women lose their virginity. Virginity is a state in which a person didn't have intercourse yet. That's why waiting for the right love to experience it is essential."

"But I would never want to hurt the girl I love."

"That's why gentleness and compassion are so important so that the first experience will be a great memory."

"Mom? Do you have to be married to have sex or have a baby?"

"A century ago, the social norm was to marry before you had sexual intercourse. Divorce was also not permitted or hardly allowed. But the truth is, love and sex have nothing to do with marriage. Also, different people have different views, based on their beliefs and religious standpoints."

"Mom? Do you know what I heard? My classmate's daddy is a baby-maker doctor!!! Does it mean he has sex with women to make babies?"

'Oh, sweet child of mine, your classmate's father is

a fertility doctor. He is the one who makes it possible for some couples who are challenged to conceive a baby."

"How?"

"Well, with different medical procedures. There are three types of fertility treatments: medicines, surgical procedures, and assisted conception – including Intrauterine Insemination (IUI) and In Vitro Fertilization (IVF). IVF involves retrieving mature eggs from a woman, fertilizing them with a man's sperm in a dish in a lab, then transferring the embryos into the uterus after fertilization. IVF is the most effective assisted reproductive technology," Uma explained. "Fertility treatment typically refers to medications that stimulate egg or sperm production, or Pro Fertility treatment typically refers to medications that stimulate egg or sperm production or procedures that involve the handling of eggs, sperm, or embryos. Understand?"

"Wow, that is cool. I wanted to be a brain surgeon, but maybe I will become a fertility doctor. Do you think I can become a fertility doctor?"

"If that's what would make you happy!"

"I just really love science! You are such a smart mommy. I want to be like you. I love you!"

"More than you know! All right, darling, it's enough for today. I want you to close your eyes and take some deep breaths. Time for your evening grace. What are you grateful for today?"

"I am so grateful for our new baby! I am! Also, I am grateful to have you, Pappy, Granny, and Cosmo! And I am happy to have great friends. You know, mom, one of my classmates had a hole in his shoes today, and he had very little lunch to bring. I shared my food and gave him my apple and half of my sandwich. My belly was full already. He said both of his parents lost their jobs. Can we help them? Mommy?"

"I will try to reach out to the administration and help them through their challenges if they expect our help. You see, there are so many who go hungry to bed."

"Yes, I know. Oh, and I am grateful I have food to eat. Mom? I was so jealous to see our friend's huge house, I thought we were poor, but you know what? I don't think that way anymore!"

"I am glad your perspective has changed. Everything we look at is perspective. Some people measure success with money and big houses while some measure it with good friends, and journeys they take, traveling or education. A big house is not always filled with love and harmony. Remember, baby boy; there is always someone who has more money, who is more intelligent, who has a bigger boat, who is quicker! You don't need to compete with anyone but yourself. If you love what you have, I assure you will be happy. Success means nothing if you are not at peace with yourself. And try not to complain; it makes you focus on the negative. There is even a song about it; that says if you complain, you pray for the devil .. something like it.

Now, no more talking. Time for your night meditation. Which one do you want to listen to?"

"The friendly whale would be just perfect tonight. Thanks, Mom! I love you, and I love you, Daddy, too!

"Love you, stinky face. Good night!" Papi kissed him good night.

Chapter Three

Kindness Matters

Days, weeks, and months went by. Uma's belly got bigger and bigger! She was exhausted and couldn't wait to see her new baby's face! They found out along the way that they would have another son, and they all were joyous!

When Simon asked his mom what she preferred to have, she always replied that as long as the baby was healthy, it didn't matter! So did his father! Simon always heard his mom say health is wealth, which he initially didn't understand.

"You know, when you are ill, you cannot go to practice piano, neither goes to play soccer or walk the puppy. Just like adults, they can't perform at work or home if they are sick. They need to hire help and pay for it, or they won't get paid at work, so their income will be less. That's where this expression comes from."

"Hm... I get it now, mommy."

"How was school today? Did you play a lot?"

"The teachers took away our recess again because some children were behind with their math studies. Mrs. Loony said she has much pressure from the district and wants us to succeed on the tests. But mom, I think I got in trouble, and they might have to go to the red carpet." (Uma often referred to the parent-teacher conference as the red carpet)

"Why do you think you are in trouble?"

"I told Mrs. Loony, 'Excuse me, Mrs. Loony, but I think it is unfair to take our recess away. We work hard, and we need to go and run a little bit. Mom, I do better when I get some breaks between classes. Am I in trouble?"

"Were you polite and respectful when you talked to your teacher?"

"Of course, mom, I am always nice."

"I prefer you to be kind. Being kind is honest while being nice is not necessarily; it could be pretending."

"Yes, mom, I had manners," Simon giggled.

"So, you are not in trouble with me or your father. Let them call me. I agree with you. You, kids, need recess and play. Testing is not the most important thing in life. Compassion, kindness, and knowledge through experiences are! Talking about the experience, I signed us up for community gardening."

"What is that?"

"We will get a small part from the city's garden, where we can plant our organic seeds, and we can share and swap them with others. Before we go to the garden, we have to go to the animal shelter. I think walking those poor souls is a great activity!"

"I want to take them all, mommy!"

"You need to understand that we cannot afford to adopt more dogs, but we can make a difference by collecting beds, walking them, and buying them food. Collecting used doggy beds and blankets also helps the earth. We upcycle, and it won't end on the land field. The world would be much better if everybody contributed as much as we do."

"What will you say to the principal if they call you?"

"I will tell them how grateful we are for their hard work and passion. I will also tell them I strongly agree with my genius little son and will ensure we all are on the same page regarding the importance of recess."

"Thanks, mom, for having my back!"

"I will always be your advocate, but you must promise never to bend the truth or break our trust with lies. Remember, I can only help if I know every detail."

"I promise, mom. Even if it's something bad or embarrassing?"

"Even then! Trust is the most crucial thing in any relationship. It's so hard to build and so easy to destroy with dishonesty. You were polite and respectful and stood up for yourself and your class. I am proud of you!"

"But great grandpa Michael said it's necessary to lie sometimes! He said it saved his life in the war, and sometimes, he tells white lies to Grandma Vanda if she asks him about her weight. For example, if Granny Vanda asks Grandpa Michael, 'Do you think I lost weight? He will say 'yes' to keep the peace even if he thinks she didn't. I think peace is important, mom."

"Oh no! My crazy old man," she giggled! "Only if it saves our life, do you understand?"

"I guess I do."

"Simon, today we will visit your friend in the hospital! I have to make sure you are ready to see her. She is unfortunately not doing well anymore. She has lost much weight and cannot walk anymore."

"I cannot wait to see her! Can she speak? Can I read stories for her?"

"Yes, she still speaks, but she is tired a lot. I think she would be happy if you could read for her."

"I will bring my Harry Potter book. I know Nickole loves it."

They arrived at the St. Joseph hospital, where Nickole had spent the last eight months. She had a sporadic genetic disease that was incurable - Stoneman syndrome. It is a congenital disease when the ligaments and joints get hardened, and excess appears on the body, with short life acceptance.

"Do you think she will be fine one day? You said it is incurable. Will she die, Mommy?" Simon asked with teary eyes.

His mother also teared up, just thinking of the possibility of losing her friend's little girl.

"There is always hope, darling. There is always new technology, and the medical field is improving quickly, so maybe if she made it this far… but as it is now, the doctors say there is not much they can do except relieve her pain. But my lovely, let's stay positive. Our mission with these visitations is to cheer her up as much as possible."

They walked toward the room where Simon 's little friend resided, but Simon started to be slower and slower. He hesitated and even ceased before he entered the room. Her mother patiently waited till he got ready to reunite with his friend. He took a deep breath, put a big smile on his face, and finally entered.

Nickole was happy to see them. She had a better day, and Simon talked a lot with her. She was a very smart little kid and had a great sense of humor. She understood her time on earth was limited and tried to cheer everyone around her.

After a while, Nickole asked Simon to push her in the wheelchair to the cafeteria because she was starving. She craved some yummy hospital hamburger! By the time they strolled to the cafe, other friends had arrived. After lunch, they decided to do a wheelchair race at Nickole's request.

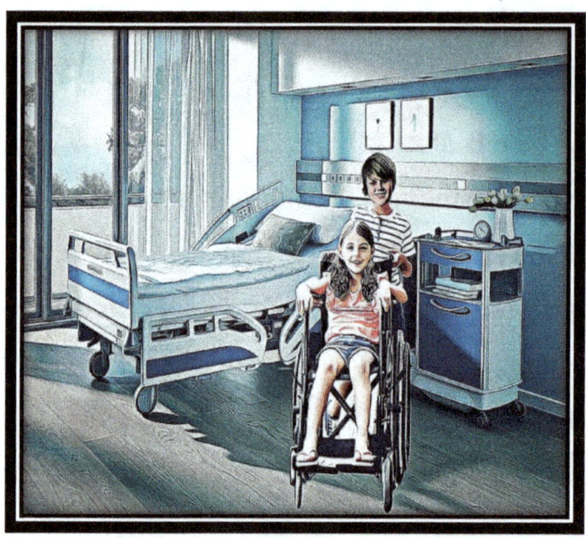

The nurses are more forgiving in a hospital where permanently ill children reside. It's almost like they try to let their wishes come true every day, within the safety protocols, of course. The hospital was far away, so they stayed until Nickole was ready to have her afternoon sleep. All the kids were playing with her. Some played board games and some chess, and some girls painted art and hung it on the wall. They watched the nurses and doctors do their jobs, change the IV, draw blood, and give her medicines. "It is hard to watch," said a little girl.

When they left, Simon remained quiet. He didn't want to talk at all, which was very unusual. Uma didn't force the conversation; she only ensured she was there if he needed to speak.

Upon their arrival, the silly dachshund greeted them at home with loud barking while jumping around. Even if Simon was mentally drained, he took the puppy for a walk with his dad. Upon their return, Uma set the table and prepared for supper while Papi cooked some delicious veggie lasagna again. The food was inviting, smelled, and tasted great! Simon's father was vegetarian for a long time. It meant he didn't eat meat. Mama Uma was only temporarily vegetarian. Because of her pregnancy, she couldn't stand the smell of meat. On the other hand, Simon loved his steak!

"Mom? Am I a bad person?"

"What? Why would you be bad?"

"So many people don't eat meat. Many people are vegetarians. And I really love steak!"

"You are not bad because you love to eat meat. Humans are meat eaters. Our ancestors gathered and hunted! The way we treat animals is bad. The factory farming industry is bad. We do not respect what we eat. They're often given so little space that they can't even turn around or lie comfortably. Egg-laying hens are kept in small cages, chickens and pigs in jam-packed sheds, and cows in crowded, filthy feedlots," Uma explained. "Antibiotics are used to make animals grow faster and to keep them alive. Most factory-farmed animals have been genetically manipulated to grow larger or to produce more milk or eggs than they naturally would. That has to change, and it can't go any further. And do you know animals create most of the carbon monoxide with their waste?"

"With their poop, you mean?"

"Yes, with their poop. Also, how we deforest enormous jungles to have more factory farms has to be changed."

"But I don't destroy jungles nor hurt animals like that!"

"Did you ever hear that you vote with your money? You do not buy conventional meat when you decide you won't support big industrial farming. Instead, you buy food from your farmers and farmer's markets or grow your food. That's when you make a difference."

"When I eat my meat, I do not think of the cow or chicken, but if they would show me my food alive, I don't think I could eat it. Thank God daddy made zucchini lasagna today," he sighed.

That night he prayed for Nickole and the forests around the world! He couldn't fall asleep, so he asked his mother to stay with him that night. She granted his wish, comforted him, and they both fell numb holding hands.

Chapter Four

Welcome Matt!

Two weeks later, Uma was gardening and felt a sharp pain in her pelvis. She got worried and called for her husband in a petrified voice. It wasn't her time yet to deliver the baby since she was only 36 weeks into her pregnancy, and usually, a healthy pregnancy is due between 38-40 weeks, which is about nine months.

It was Sunday morning, and everybody was home. Uma walked into the house and called her midwife. Simon drew a tub of baths for her mom because she wished to deliver the baby at home in a bathtub, just like she wanted with Simon. The midwife was worried, so she told Uma to go to the hospital to ensure everything was fine with her son. She followed the instructions and trusted her midwife and doula.

"Mom, are you going to be ok? And what about my baby brother?"

"Yes, I promise, and you promise me you will listen to granny Grace and go to bed on time."

The parents returned from the hospital within 2 hours. It was a false alarm. Uma had Braxton hick, an imitation of labor contractions without going into actual labor.

A few weeks passed, and Uma's belly looked like a giant watermelon. She was tired and wanted to get her baby out. The whole family was impatient. Simon was very excited and couldn't wait to meet his baby brother. One day after he got home from school, he found her mother sitting on a big blue ball in the living room. Granny Grace was massaging Uma's back.

His mother turned to him and said, "Your brother is ready to meet us soon. Will you please let the water run in the bathtub?"

Simon turned the water on immediately. "Mom, shouldn't you go to the hospital?" he asked Uma.

"Not yet. I will have a warm, comforting bath and wait until I feel it's time to go. Go and bring me some chilled hibiscus and raspberry leaf, mint tea, and tell daddy to make me an arugula salad with fresh pineapple. It will help me with my dilation."

"Dial what?" he asked.

"My cervix needs to dilate. You know to be able to push your brother through the birth canal. Go on and get my tea, please."

Simon ran down the stairs. She was listening to them

singing in the kitchen while preparing her launch. After a while, they both returned, serving her tea. Papi asked Uma gently if it was time to go, but she replied no. The hospital was nearby, so they were not in a hurry. Just like Simon's birth, Uma had a detailed birth plan, but God had a different plan for her firstborn.

"Mommy? Who did you talk to when we came back with your lunch? Were you on a zoom call with your patient? Because I heard a deep male voice telling you to breathe deeply!"

(Uma was a Silva method graduate and practiced visualization and self-hypnosis to deal with stress from her work. This is a technique to rewrite negative thinking and lead a successful, healthy life.)

"No, it was my birth hypnosis. It helps me to relax and focus, just like when you do your guided meditation before going to sleep.

"Why is it good for us to meditate, mommy?"

"It helps you relieve stress and stay focused. Visualization is deeply empowering. It helps you create your reality."

"Oh, all right, I get it now, but the man's voice in your hypnosis is weird. I prefer my treehouse mediation."

Simon stopped talking for a while and gazed at his

mother's face in silence before he asked, "Where is the baby coming out from?"

'From the birth canal, through the vagina. Do you remember when I told you? I needed raspberry leaf tea to help me dilate. It is a long process when the birth canal expands so that the mommies can push their babies through. The cervix has to be 10cm big. But every woman is different. We all give birth in different ways. Some have vaginal birth through the birth canal; some have C-sections. C-section is a shorter term for cesarean surgery. Some have short and less painful births, and some experience long and painful births. You can schedule a C-section if you choose to. One of my classmates had her baby at home in 45 minutes in her birth tub. I called her a freak of nature," she smiled.

"Good for her. Most mommies have longer births."

'Can you get medicine for your pain?"

'Yes, you can get different pills or gas, laughing gas just like what you had at the dentist or an epidural. Epidural is an injection, they inject it in the mommy's lower back, which temporarily paralyzes the woman from the waist, so they don't feel the pain."

"Aren't you sleeping during the surgery?"

'No, not necessarily. You can be up unless it's a terrible complication. You can ask for an epidural during vaginal birth also."

"Can you, mom? Can you? Please! I don't want you to be in pain. I love you."

"Time will tell. I might be just fine. All women have different pain levels," answered his mother.

"Are you in pain now?"

"I only have a very low discomfort yet, so I can answer more questions if you have any."

"Mom, I always have questions. How was I born? I love when you talk about my childhood."

"Childhood? What do you think you are now? You are still a little boy to me."

"No, mom, I am not anymore. I will be a big brother soon."

"I remember being so excited and couldn't wait to meet you. I hired a doula and a midwife, just like with your little brother right now (midwives and doulas are medically trained women who help during birth). I had a birth plan; I chose my favorite reggae music, an entire playlist of what your father played for me every night, while I bathed. Your father is the most nurturing, romantic man in this world."

"Oh, that's why I like reggae music because you listened to it while I was in your womb?"

"Most likely," his mother smiled and continued.

"The morning I went into labor, I was walking on the beach. The other words for giving birth are labor and delivery. I rushed home and sat in the water just like now. Six hours later, we went to the hospital because we lived on an island where they didn't allow us to give birth at home. My labor was 40 hours long, and we had an emergency cesarean because your little head got tilted. I didn't choose it, but it was necessary to survive! Some women choose to have c-sections, and it's all fine. All moms want what 's best for their babies."

"Wait a minute … an emergency? To survive? Can you die?"

"We will be just fine, do not worry! But did you know I was stillborn? Stillborn means when the baby dies in the womb or during labor! But a young medic started to give me CPR, and here I am! My story ended happily, but not everybody is lucky as we were with granny Grace. Some women or babies die during labor."

"I am so glad you were lucky. I could never imagine another mommy. I would never love another mommy."

Silence... there was a deep silence after that until Simon spoke again.

"Did it hurt? The surgery? Did it hurt?"

"After the surgery, it did."

"After? How is it even possible?"

"It's major surgery. The wound has to heal, and it heals slowly. But you can take pain medication if you choose to."

"So, when you had the Caesar salad cut on your belly, were we in danger?"

"It's not Caesar salad, silly-Billy. It 's cesarean." Uma laughed so hard she even peed herself a bit! It's common before birth because the baby is pressing on the bladder. "I know it 's a lot of new words you've got introduced to today. If you don 't understand something, let me know; otherwise, please ask your father. I think it 's time to go."

"Can I go, please?"

His parents decided to gently decline his request in case of an emergency.

"You will need to obey granny Grace and make sure she is comfortable. She doesn't speak English. You will be her translator, all right?"

"I promise! I miss you already, mommy."

"How can you miss me while I stand before you?"

"I will…." he teared up. He had never been away from his mother. As much as he loved his granny, he felt a little sad.

Uma had a V-BAC, which means vaginal birth after

a C-section. She gave birth in a birth tub and welcomed her newborn son, Matt. Simon visited the hospital with granny Grace to visit Uma and his little brother. Simon was thrilled to meet Matt. He loved his chubby little face; he sang for him and read his favorite books.

Papi stayed with Matt and Uma in the hospital. Two days later, the whole family reunited in their home. Matt was not so quiet little boy; he cried a lot from some belly discomfort. Uma fed him with breast milk.

"We call it breastfeeding or nursing," Uma explained to Simon.

"Mommy, mommy, cover your breast. It's spraying all over, just like a sprinkle in the garden."

"Oh no, it's sprayed, daddy," he laughed.

"What is that noisy thing on your breast?"

"It's a breast pump," Papi answered him. "It helps pump out all the milk so that it can reproduce again for the baby. It also helps me to bond with Matt. Men don't produce breast milk, so mom pumps, and we can store it in the fridge for later. At night, granny or I can take turns feeding and letting mommy sleep a little.

"But we have nothing else in the fridge but breastmilk," Papi commented grumpily. "I might have to put it in a smoothie to make some space for fish."

"Well, mother's milk is considered gold," Uma replied.

"So, you are a millionaire, Uma!" said granny Grace while laughing hysterically.

"Everybody nurses their babies?" continued the little boy.

"No, some can't produce, and some choose not to."

"But why, if this is the best you can do for your baby?

"We can't judge. Life is complicated. Some women choose to return to work, and some have no choice but to do so because they have no stable financial support. I am truly blessed to have your father's support and for my work. I could always work from home and be there for you guys. Some women choose not to nurse their babies because of vanity. They don't want to sacrifice the beauty of their breasts. It can get saggy during nursing and with aging. However, babies can be bottle-fed with formula. It's a scientifically created powder with vitamins that you dissolve in water that perfectly nurtures the baby's developmental needs."

"When did you stop breastfeeding me? I don't remember."

"That's good you don't," giggled Uma. "I weaned you when you became 26 months old. I was exhausted and very uncomfortable. Most children wean themselves naturally between 1-3 years. Some women go to an excessive time of 7-8 years."

"Oh no, oh no, mommy! I would never want that. It's embarrassing! You go to school and still nursed? Why?" he made a disgusting smirk on his face.

"I don't know the answers to everything."

"You should. You are a therapist," he said.

"Well, all right. Some women live in countries where they lack food, and until they can produce milk, they will nourish their children with it. Some have disabled children who refuse to eat solid food. However, breast milk quality keeps changing during the first two years. First, it stops producing colostrum. Then it will lack fat and even protein. It drastically decreases nutrition, so it does not positively impact a child after a while. Some women, I guess, try to have a baby for so long that when it happens, they can't let go of babying them. That is an extraordinary, strong emotional bond between mother and child, and it's tough for both to let it go most of the time." Uma explained. "I know some women who breastfed their kids till they turned 7."

Chapter Five

Wisdom – Better Than Smart

Years went by, and the boys grew so much. They loved to play lacrosse and learned how to play piano and drum. They both started to compete in dance. They even chose a song that became their hymn, that inspired them right before each competition; Sky is the limit by Rebolution.

Simon chose ballroom, while Matt opted for hip-hop. They were blessed with their coaches and always found the best!

One afternoon when Uma was driving them to their activities, she was dying from laughter listening to her two geniuses talking in the back seat.

Simon: Matt, you are so immature! I am afraid you would still go with a kidnapper if they would show you a cute puppy!

Matt: You would be surprised. I have changed, and I am the second strongest in class; I would kick them in the nuts!

Simon: Hm yeah, sometimes people surprise us! Do you remember mom's red high heels? Anyway, I found some comfort in that shoe! I was convinced that if an intruder approached us, mommy would be the one who would disarm them, not dad. But actually, I started to realize daddy might surprise us! He is stronger than we think!

Matt: Hm, yes, mommy is feisty. She was yelling at the speeding cars today! Out in public! (Simon said with a facepalm)

Simon: Yes, she can be truly sassy! Anyway, do you know what to do if they want to kidnap you?

Matt: What?

Simon: You got to limp; it's adding 100 pounds to your weight, and the best option is to soil yourself! I heard that in Grace and Frankie!

Matt: What does soil yourself mean?

Simon: Oh, Matt! You have to shit yourself so they won't want to touch you and go for the clean ones!

They were hilarious little boys who made their parents laugh frequently.

Matt: Mom, I read about the fountain of youth in St. Augustine. The story says if you sprinkle water on your face, you stay forever young! I don't remember doing it during our visit.

Uma: I got a great story about it. Before you were born, I went with dad, and paper cups were offered to drink from the fountain of youth! And I did! But I had such a horrible stomach ache with diarrhea. It was excruciating!

Matt (walked up to his mom and hugged her): Poor mommy, you had to endure so much pain, and it didn't even work.

Uma and Papi continued radical honesty with their parenting, choosing the right words to ensure the answers suited their kids' current stage of development. And you can imagine, they always had questions, just like you, who read this book. They were curious boys. Some questions were challenging for Uma and Papi, and some shouldn't have been answered.

It was a sunny Thursday afternoon when Simon came home from school and told her mom they had quite a nasty incident in class. It was a human reproduction class led by a male teacher. The teacher was drunk and very inappropriate in answering the kids' questions.

"How inappropriate?" asked Uma.

"Well, some children who weren't discussing sex at home started to cry. I heard they were assigned to the school therapist."

"Oh my! That bad? What happened?"

He hesitated to answer for a while and then asked, "Mom, what is masturbation?"

"Wow, all right," Uma thought. It was time to talk about this anyway. "Masturbation is stimulation of one's genitals, either the clitoris or penis."

"What is a dildo or vibrator?"

"Ok, that's not something we need to address in school. However, I will tell you. It's a tool, a sex tool. Different tools are used during sex or masturbation to achieve pleasure. Why? What did he say?"

"Same, but he encouraged everyone to snoop in their mother's drawer because all women use one."

"That is false. Not all women. It's a fact."

"How about porn?"

Uma got infuriated but tried not to express her disappointment and kept answering.

"It's a staged sex scene. A video that other people can watch. It can wrongly influence a young adult's approach to a healthy sex life, so I would not recommend it. Anything else?"

"Yes," Simon said. "He told us he does not like to use protection for safe sex; he rather has the women use it."

"Oh no! Oh no, that's it! I am calling your father, and we are going back to school! By the way, you never leave your reproduction rights in anybody's hands. Latex condoms are the most common birth protection. They can prevent unwanted pregnancies and prevent sexually transmitted diseases. Women can use pills or patches that increase some hormones to avoid pregnancy. On the other hand, men can choose vasectomy, a surgical procedure that stops the supply of sperm to their semen. You always protect yourself even if a girl says she is on pills. Do you understand?" Uma paused and asked, "Did he say anything else?"

"Mom, I just can't say it! You got to ask other parents."

His parents stormed back to school and realized 30 other aggravated parents were waiting for the principal to show her face. The teacher was removed immediately on the parents' demand and prosecuted later.

"It only takes one bad teacher to ruin it all for them," said Uma to Papi. That night she couldn't sleep a wrinkle. She heard a lot of disturbing facts and was tossing herself, rolling from one side to the other, back and forth. Then she remembered one of her patient's stories. A young woman had a neighbor, and they had about the same old kid. Both were five years old boys. They often had playdates. Uma's patient claimed to have cameras all over her home, so she could follow the boys anywhere while playing.

One day, they went to have a playdate at her neighbor's house. The boys went together to the bathroom to pee, with open doors. The mother of the other child saw them touch each other's penis for a second. They claimed the client's son to be the initiator and blamed her and her husband for that incident. Her neighbor based her opinion on her interrogation of her son. When Uma asked her patient if she questioned her son, she answered, "My son explained he was curious because he had never seen a circumcised penis before."

Uma's patient's male members did not choose to be circumcised (circumcision is a relatively simple procedure. The foreskin is removed just behind the head of the penis using a scalpel or surgical scissors.)

"Why do men circumcise?" Uma's patient questioned her.

"Not every man is circumcised. Sometimes there are medical needs for it (foreskin retraction also reduces sexually transmitted infections), and sometimes religious beliefs are involved." Uma explained to her devastated patient. "It is a natural curiosity to know what other children have. Neither one of the five years old can be a valid source of information."

Uma's patient started to cry and said, "My son has a

spectrum, and he can't even lie."

She was genuinely hurt and disappointed. She cursed and said irrelevant things like she still breastfeeds a kindergartener.

"Come on now, whose family is awkward?"

Uma advised the lady to distance herself from her neighbor's family and told her there was no reason to accuse any five years old. But that night, she couldn't sleep. She realized she needed to talk to her younger son.

The following day during breakfast, she adjusted some issues. Usually, they played trivia or chose your poison during breakfast and dinner, but today she just cut to the chase.

"All right, boys, nobody can touch your penis or look at your penis unless it's your pediatrician and only if either daddy or I am present. It doesn't matter whether you are a boy or a girl. It affects both genders."

Uma was sexually abused when she was a little girl. She was a very aware mommy because of her trauma. Probably that was the underlying reason she became a psychiatrist and talked openly about everything with her boys.

'Sexual abuse is when someone forces intercourse on someone without their consent," Uma explained. "It's called rape. Molestation is when someone is being touched inappropriately. When an adult does any of these actions with a child, we call it a pedophile. It's all against the law, and those people must be prosecuted and incarcerated and at least should be sent to prison for life. However, if I ever would become a president, I would make sure to execute them"

"Mummy, is our neighbor across the street a pedophile? You know Mr. Tail, who always has his penis hanging out of his shorts."

"No darling, he is a disgusting old flasher. Daddy already talked to him and warned him to be reported to the police if we see it one more time."

The boys planned their morning sailing out for fishing with their father, which was one of their favorite activities with their dad.

"It's so hard to parent these days," Uma complained to her grandmother, Vanda, when she Facetimed her. Her paternal grandmother was her favorite, a sage woman who had just turned 90. "I don't know if I did it right or if I was constantly making mistakes. The technology! Should I let them use it or not? There is so much content on YouTube that has no value at all, and I am sure it makes them dumber every time they watch it. How about their friends? Should I choose them? The activities are overwhelming!"

Uma's grandmother was not an educated woman. She had to stop studying when World War II escalated in Europe. Nonetheless, she was an experienced old lady.

"It is always hard. Parenting is one of the most challenging jobs one can have. After having a baby, you wear your heart on your sleeve," she responded to Uma's complaints. "You will make mistakes… many mistakes. We all did. But make sure your heart is in the right place, and your intention is good. That's all that matters. You young women want to compete whose children know more, whose children started to walk earlier and talk earlier. Does it really matter? Stop trying to impress others! When you get older, you will understand. You will wish you wouldn't rush the time. Look at the trees. It's as if they know what is going on. You cannot rush the trees to change their leaves. You can't hurry nature, and still, everything is done that needs to be done. Why do you want them to speak three languages when they have no place to practice them? And about the friends… you choose until they are capable of making great choices. Friends define us, and it is crucial to teach them early on. Choose a friend you can look up to and who completes you."

"You are such an amazing human. I wish you could

be with me forever," sighed the young mother.

"You are brilliant yourself," Vanda continued. "You should know nothing stays forever. Nothing! Everything changes, just like the leaves change colors every autumn, and that is how it is supposed to be - the circle of life: conception and death. And, of course, joy, a lot of laughter and joy,"

"I wish to be like you. It feels like I just collected so many master's degrees which only get dusty on the shelves. Matt told me today that he doesn't want to go to university and wants to be a YouTuber. He wants to be a millionaire, and I stop him from being one. I was so upset. I raise them with high values, with integrity, and I find intelligence very important."

Vanda laughed again. "They can have it all without having a master's degree, you know? I am not saying I don't value education. I wanted to be an art teacher, and you know that, but I did not have a chance. But also, I never gave up on painting. It never kept me from becoming an artist."

Uma was listening to Damien Marley's song in the background when they both heard him sing, "wisdom *better than smart*," and they started to laugh at the same time.

"There is the sign you are always looking for," joked Vanda.

"I need to hang up, grandma. The boys will be back soon."

Chapter Six

Ying to My Yang!

The family went for a walk that night. Before the sunset, the sky was mesmerizing! It was ten minutes before seven. The temperature dropped significantly. A mysterious haze started to appear, and the sky dressed up in a colorful costume! It looked like cotton candy! Wait! No! It looked like Bob Ross had begun to paint a renaissance midnight summer ball, and his paint buckets all tipped over! They were granted this beauty quite often. They kept walking until they got intoxicated by this vision. Soon, the dark sky crawled up on them, and the spectacular moon, coupled with sparkly Venus, kept their company!

Months later, Matt came home from school very disturbed. He was seemingly upset.

"What's wrong," his father asked.

"It's bad. My friend Donovan…the children called him a dummy and fat! One even said the 'N-word."

The parents froze. Papi asked if any teacher was present.

"No," Matt said. "But I told on them, and they called me a snitch. I love Donovan. He is my best friend. His heart is made from gold, and he is truly a gentle giant."

'Do you remember the song?" he started humming it,

"Why should I be afraid of you when you bleed just like I do' by Jesse Royal?"

'Of course, it is one of my favorites," Matt shouted excitedly.

"We all have the same inside. The color of our skin should not define us…Ever! We all have dreams, and we all have secrets. We all make mistakes, and we all want to be happy. We are glad you told the teachers, it is intolerable, and we are proud of you."

'But they won't like me anymore. They called me a rat!"

'You can't please everyone," Uma replied. 'You had chosen wisely. You did it out of love and not for the likes. He is your best friend, and you stood up for him, which is very courageous."

'Mom, I can even use my tegatana-ganmen-uchi karate strike on them."

'Please don't," said Papi. 'Karate is for defense, not for offense. I will make sure to talk to your teachers tomorrow and express our disappointment."

'But why are they saying things like that? It is rude

and hurtful."

"Duality is imprinted in our genes. We are all capable of doing both good and bad. It is a choice we need to make every day. But remember, most kids have no idea what they are saying. They do not necessarily understand the word; they just copy their peers or something they heard on social media. Some are insecure and need to hurt others to feel better about themselves. And some are just simply…Evil," Papi finished Uma 's sentence.

"Papi, what exactly does the "N" word mean? I know it 's bad, and we can 't say it, but I have no clue! What is it?"

Pappi went on Google and started to read Wikipedia:

"Nigger is derived from the Latin word for the color black, niger, in Spanish it's negro. It is an extremely hateful, ethnic slur, offensive, racist word for black people."

"Words have tremendous weight. It can lift you or destroy you," continued his mother.

"Mom, what if some of my African American classmates say I have the pass for the 'N-word?"

"What? Oh no!!! Never, ever, ever dare to say that. Do you understand?"

"I see, mom. But why does Mr. Ludo use the word?"

"I bet he is ignorant and doesn 't even know its meaning. Anyway, I think he is one of them. He is racist."

The Shuster family had their share of experience being bullied for t. Uma was not very good at controlling her emotions regarding her kids.

"A monk can t shave his own head," she often said.

She couldn't give credible advice to herself. She wanted to be the shelter for them forever, but she knew they would eventually need to protect themselves.

Her 90-year-old grandma used to say, "You make sure you are there when they need to stand up again. You can t cry their tears. You can t fight their battles. Just stand tall and strong, so whenever they are ready to stand on their own again, you will be their support to hold onto."

It is tough to see your children struggle. Uma felt angry and often wanted revenge. One day, she learned that Simon was bullied in school both verbally and physically by other kids. She was saddened and extremely angry at the same time! At first, he was called gay, faggot, and tinkle toes! His mother said she would report this to the school administration. Simon asked his mother not to get involved yet. He assured her he would take care of it! Uma found comfort in his confidence and thought it had stopped there. But it didn't*!*

Simon's success was the soil of being bullied frequently. The name calls were nothing. He was advised to kill himself because nobody would miss him. One of the aggressors was a girl (whose mother worked at school as a launch guard). This young girl kicked Simon over and over again and bruised his body repeatedly. Then she made fun of him, saying, "You bruise just like a girl, man up!"

Uma asked him, "Why on earth wouldn't you kick back?"

He'd been told to respect others, so he answered, "Girls are fragile."

"This one is not," his mother sighed, irritated.

Uma couldn't understand why he never mentioned it. They used to have fantastic communication between them. The young boy admitted he covered it up because he wouldn't want to sadden his mother, who had two lost pregnancies; one was a recent ectopic pregnancy due to which she struggled with her health. Ectopic pregnancy is when the ovum fertilizes in the fallopian tube and raptures it later. She had to go to the ER and was really sick for weeks.

The school police and the district got involved, but the girl had a great backwind, so she wasn't paying the proper consequences for her actions. Unfortunately, the school administration hasn't had a strong backbone.

They victimized the aggressor and blamed the victims. However, the girl had to apologize and ask for

Simon 's forgiveness.

He said, 'Sometimes things that are said and done cannot be forgiven! You not only bruised my body, but you wounded my soul! I will never forget that!"

Simon was bothered by the fact that children thought of him being gay, not because there was anything wrong with being gay.

The school had changed so much. Access to the internet lets young children seek answers, but unfortunately, they don 't necessarily look in the right place. Many children have no privilege to ask their parents because it 's considered taboo, surrounded by hazy guilt. Simon and Matt were lucky. Their parents always talked about everything and made them aware of society's different types of people.

There are so many groups, some even his parents didn't know about. The asexual (not wanting to have sex), the transgender (changing their gender through surgery), the pansexual who loves all, non-binary, gender-fluid, and the furries pretending to be animals.

"What do you mean they pretend to be animals?" his father asked with a heavy accent.

"They dress like foxes or rabbits, and their parents play along," answered Simon.

Papi was disturbed.

'So, the parent 's let them be foxes? Are they living in the wood, hunting their food, and fighting off the stronger predators for survival? If not, people who want to be identified by animals should take theatre classes or come for a therapy session with your mom, Simon. And by the way, can any of you explain to me how on earth one can be an asexual when one is not even active sexually yet? Were you aware of those things, Uma?"

She nodded with a yes.

"And did you mention they want to be called different pronouns?" his father couldn't stop asking questions.

'I cannot get this," he kept shaking his head.

'So, if a female decides she is a 'him 'instead of a 'she 'or a motorcycle or a shark, I need to use that as a pronoun. This is sick!"

'Simon, we came from a different country. In our native language, we don 't have any differences in pronouns. Ten years of my life in America, I have been corrected to use the right pronouns because they didn't stick. Finally, I used it correctly, and you are saying I did it for nothing? After mastering it, I cannot use the correct grammar because some will get offended!

"Gender fluid? What does that even mean? Do you

think children in third-world countries have time to argue about this shit? This is insane!"

Papi became angry and sad. He became all grumpy and continued his monologue. "I was reading the other day that they accept children going under medical castration. Children who are so young! Their frontal lobe has not developed yet, so they cannot make a responsible decision about something critical like this. Once it's done, it cannot be reversed."

"Well, there are only two genders, boys. It's decided very early on the first moment of conception," Uma took the lead. "The XY chromosome makes a person a male, and the XX chromosome makes someone a female."

"That's it! It does not make you a fan, a motorcycle, a cat, or anything else. Male and female, that's it. I can strongly advise that someone attracted to sharks or thinks they are cats, dogs, or motorcycles should seek psychiatric help. This is mental illness," their mother lectured them patiently.

"I hope you guys are confident enough not to be pressured by others. It's ok not to belong. I have always been a mysterious, misunderstood boy, but I never felt the need to follow the crowd," their father said.

Simon assured his parents he was not pressured.

Indeed, he dared to ask some of his female peers why they thought he was gay.

The answer deeply disappointed both of his parents. Apparently, because he was ballroom dancing and was kind and polite.

"You are way too kind compared to other boys; one young girl told him."

Listening to what Simon said made his father's eyes fill with tears.

"I can't believe we are raising two kind-hearted, romantic gentlemen with values, and that's how society appreciates it. He is being punished for being kind!"

"I told you to stop saying girls are fragile because some aren't, and it can be a major problem for them later," his wife replied.

"No, it's not! I still think you should not hit back at a girl. You are my queen, and I could never imagine you being hurt."

"Hm, I strongly disagree. They are still kids with the same strength, height, and weight. If you get punched multiple times as a little boy from a little girl, you just have to stand still and take it? I don't think so. I am dealing with much domestic abuse in my practice, and you would be surprised, 35% of my patients are males abused by females,"

Uma continued.

"What about the young black college student accused of rape? Court? Jail? They could prove it was a false accusation a year later, but he lost his college football team privilege and a year of his life. The woman is roaming free with no accountability for her action. The best part is that she was in love with this young guy, who rejected her love. These matters are not supposed to be based on and justified by gender, skin color, religion, or nationality. Simply soul hurt soul based. Everything else is insignificant! Papi, you better talk to the boys about this. Simon told me one little girl who had a crush on him wanted to close the door at the Halloween party to kiss him."

"Don't worry, I already have," answered her husband. "Do you know what is so interesting, darling?" continued Papi.

"The boys don't stand up for themselves but always protect others. They are not bystanders when someone else vulnerable is being mistreated. Simon just told me two days ago that he has a peer in the second period in his speech and debate class who has a disability. One of his legs is shorter, and the parents, who have English barriers, could not get the right special shoe for him.

Other kids called him 'limpy-dimpy,' short leg. He

went up to the cool kids and defended his peer with disabilities. He even asked me if I could do something about it. I then talked to a company willing to provide for this boy's needs."

"I am proud of you! You are a good man. Yin to my yang," said

Chapter Seven
It's Not a Talk to You Later –
It's a Goodbye

That afternoon, Uma called her grandma Vanda again. She was not in great health anymore and had trouble holding long conversations. The young woman portrayed the last two weeks of her family life.

"Grandma, I want them to be supportive and kind and stand up for others, but I don't want them to be heroes! I can't believe I am saying this. Every day I let them go to school. I tell them I love them, but don't be a hero! I don't need a pledge. I need my boys to be alive. There are so many school shootings. It is insane. Simon wanted to go to the mall with his friend, and I didn't let him because of the shootings. He debated with me and told me the statistics. He keeps arguing with me and even said it is 20% more likely to be shot at school than at a mall," Uma paused a bit, hearing the silence from the other end of the phone. "You are so quiet today…Gran? How are you?"

"I think I am ready. I don't have much time. I feel it…I will go soon, baby girl. Remember, I will always be in your heart..."

Uma made peace with it because her grandma had a love-filled life. She will selfishly miss their conversations, but she had no doubt she would live in her heart forever.

"I need to go to sleep. It's late here," Vanda said. "It's not a 'talk to you later,' it's a goodbye, my darling."

"Never stop loving you," said Uma while crying quietly. "Until we meet again."

That night Grandma Vanda said farewell to the world. She most definitely got her wings; she was an earth angel already.

The next day, early afternoon, the young woman sat by the pool drinking her coffee…She tried to look for signs. Before Vanda passed away, she told Uma that if there were an afterlife, she would send orange butterflies and tiger wing dragonflies to her.

She saw at least 20 of them that day. It made her smile.

"Mummy?" Matt's voice distracted Uma's journey back on memory lane. He held a bracelet he had made for a little girl he loved. "Do you remember when I was in preschool, and I didn't have words yet? Do you remember those three blonde-haired boys who used to punch me in the face because I couldn't say anything?"

"Hm, I remember."

"Anamaria was so nice to me. She came to my rescue. She always gathered her friends and circled me so those boys could no longer get close to me. That's why I fell in love with her forever. She is the kindest girl in this entire world. I will marry her when I grow up. I made this for her and will give it to her when she comes over."

Uma remembered very clearly. Matt's speech was delayed; he didn't talk till he turned 3.5 years old, almost 4. When somebody wrongfully treats your loved ones, it's a gut-reaping experience. She cried inside, remembering.

"She is a darling little Pisces! I agree. We all adore her!" answered his mother.

After Simon got home from school, he joined their conversation. He started a story about his Asian friend, a boy named Choi. Choi was a wealthy kid living in a lovely neighborhood. He told Simon over the weekend that their neighbor told them to move back home. He told the man that he was home and wasn't moving anywhere.

The man angrily shouted, "Tell your mother to move back to China, you fucking dirty rat!" He went into the house and told his parents what had happened.

"Never mind, mom, my friend's father is a three generational Irish American, and her mom is Korean," the boy continued.

"How did they solve the situation?" Uma asked curiously.

"His parents called the cops on the neighbor and reported to the HOA, but neither made a significant difference."

Unfortunately, bullying has become a norm. Our society accepted it. Ill-minded people project their insecurity and point fingers, blaming others for their failures. So much injustice surrounds us; we close our eyes, pretend to be blind, or turn away. So many wrong things, such as adults insulting minors, men harassing women, or women accusing men wrongfully, but we go on with our lives as if nothing is happening.

That night, Uma told the boys they would need to visit Nickole in the hospital because she was in terrible condition. She couldn't speak anymore and was bedridden.

Nickole lived to be 13, which was rare and almost impossible with her genetic disease. Her mother prolonged her life with unbelievable and exceptional, tender care and love.

The boys both respectfully declined Uma's request.

"You can't possibly expect us to go. We cannot watch her suffer anymore. I am just standing there, not capable of doing anything. Nothing mom! It makes me want to vomit from the pain. How fair is this," he yelled. "She will die, we all know. She is just a child!" Simon screamed while walking away.

Matt looked at his mother with his begging puppy eyes and asked, "Will she…Will she go to heaven, mommy?"

"We can't take away hope from anyone," Uma started to whisper." We were waiting for miracles because extraordinary things happen every day. But it does not happen to everyone. Medical technology is going through a major evolution, but I am afraid she does not have enough time to wait for it anymore."

Uma waited, paused for a while, and then said, "All right, boys, I am so sorry I ignored your feelings. I will go myself."

When she returned from the hospital, the boys asked fearfully how their little friend was doing. They saw Uma's eyes, and they knew the end was near. They asked her if they could sleep in her bed and cried themselves to sleep.

Two weeks later, they were coming home from surfing. The boys used Uma's phone to put on some music in the car. Everybody had a turn. Simon had the phone when a text came through. Nickole's father said, "Nickole no longer had the strength to fight! Her journey ended today on Earth."

Papi had to pull over because they all started to sob. That night, Matt told his parents he didn't want to pray anymore because his prayers weren't being answered.

I just want to say thank you every night, and that's that."

Nickole's funeral was held in their preschool church.

The family was there for the last ride. It was deeply heartbreaking. The boys and other children were invited to the altar, singing the last song to her.

They sang the song from Bruno Mars; Count on me.

That night they slept in their parents' room again.

"Mom?" Matt started. "I was so scared. I thought the

black box would open, and she would sit up."

Silence. Long uncomfortable silence. Uma knew it was time to talk about it. She always waited for the right time and gauged now was the time.

"All right, Let 's talk about death."

During the last five months, they experienced three deaths of people who were very dear to their hearts. Simon 's dance coach passed away unexpectedly from a bacterial infection. They were crippled by pain over and over again. The family discussed if they should seek a grief counselor, but the boys rejected it.

"We can always talk to you, mom. We don 't need a counselor."

Uma initially hesitated, but then she remembered her grandma Vanda 's words.

"If you are upset, you need to make sure you keep your hands busy. Busy hands are happy hands. Plant a garden, write a book, make some jewelry, cook a nice meal, play tennis, and I assure you the pain will have no chance to sink and poison your soul. It would still hurt but manifest in something beautiful you create."

Uma chose to start from the fundamental fact. "The truth is that death is part of our lives, and we are all going to die one day."

She paused and continued, 'Some have a short journey, some have a longer one, some can say goodbye surrounded by loved ones, and some will leave suddenly, alone. No matter how we end, the sorrow, the emptiness we leave with our final farewell for our loved ones is unbearable, shaking us to the root of our existence."

Simon was already a teen. He understood death pretty well. Matt, on the other hand, flooded his mother with questions.

"We're all going to die? Does death hurt?"

"This is one of the most challenging questions to be answered. Most people, especially children, fear death. Dying is a process that could hurt if some suffer from terminal illnesses or injuries. Some have the privilege of dying in their sleep without any pain.

But let 's see what Wikipedia says about it…."

Uma tried to approach these heavy topics scientifically first, based on Wikipedia. She started to read: "As a point in time, death would seem to refer to the moment life ends. Death is the irreversible cessation of all biological functions that sustain an organism. The remains of a former organism normally begin to decompose shortly after death. Death is an inevitable, universal process that eventually occurs in all organisms."

"Are we going to Heaven?"

"Many cultures and religions have the idea of an afterlife, and also may hold the idea of judgment of good and bad deeds in one's life," she read. "Some refer to this judgment as Heaven and Hell, some as karma. It simply means action, reaction. You get what you give; you reap what you sow. Some believe karma or heaven and hell is a misconception, thinking it's created by the privileged to keep the mass crowd in fear."

"Do you believe in the afterlife? Do you think there is karma?" the little one picked up where they left off.

"You know my favorite character from Star Wars? ¿Yoda, the wise green, wrinkled creature? He once said, 'we are not this crude matter but spiritual beings. I believe, I feel, and I know there is more…there is life after death."

"Aren't you scared to be judged for your statement?" asked the older boy.

"Well, judgment is a funny thing! You can be the nicest, sweetest pear on this earth, but there will always be someone who will loathe pears, isn't that right?"

"Indeed, but so many won't agree with you."

"As I said, many religions and nations have different beliefs. (Religion is the belief in the worship of a superhuman controlling power, especially a God. There are ten types of faithful religions for 85% of the global population: Islam, Christianity, Hinduism, Judaism, Taoism, Buddhism, Shinto, Confucianism, and Jainism.

Our truths are always a mix of our understanding and standpoint. My truth is based on my experience, and your aunt Gertrude's is based on her experience. My grandma Vanda said, 'As you get older, the less you care about others' judgment. I don't undermine anybody's beliefs; I stand for mine. I don't let anyone think for me or let their experiences create my reality, nor should you."

"And the black box? Will we all end up in that black box?" Matt resumed. He referred to the coffin as a big black box.

'No, my dear. Different cultures and religions have different farewells. Some get cremated and put the ashes in a box in a cemetery. Some spread the ashes in water. Some get buried in a coffin, while in Muslim and Jewish cultures, they get buried without a coffin on a white sheet. Indians get cremated. Native Americans believe that if you get cremated, you will get stuck and can't reincarnate. There are cultures where they dance with their dead loved ones, and they call it the last tango. In New Zealand, they sit around the one who died for a day and talk to them."

"Mom, I know you don't want to hear this, but if I go

before you, spread my ashes into the ocean, so whenever you get in, I can hug you again."

"I definitely wouldn't want to hear that, Simon. But you know what, even if I hate the heat, do the same with me."

At that moment, the boy's father entered the room. He was listening to their conversation from the living room. He said he wants his ashes to be potted in wood, with different kinds of seeds, so one strong tree could grow from it.

"Do you believe in reincarnation?" Matt could not stop questioning his mother.

"Well, there is a fact that when we die, we are all 21 grams less at the moment of death. Some say it's the last exhaled breath, and some say it's our soul. So many scientists study the afterlife and reincarnation."

"What about ghosts?" Matt carried on with the questions.

"Well, let me answer that for you, little brother," Simon said, explaining his personal experience. "One day, I wished my friend happy birthday through text, you know, the girl whose mother died and was mommy's friend? That afternoon, I was gardening and needed to take an early shower. I went into the shower and saw a woman with my eyes open. She had long ginger hair, and she was in a beautiful short white dress. I couldn't see her face. I started to scream, and I remember mom and dad running like crazy for my rescue. They did not understand, so I had to explain what had happened. Mom and dad both claim to have experiences with spirits in the past, so they told me I was safe and that spirits won't be able to harm me. Living people can be more dangerous, father said. That night we both slept in their room again. In the morning, I learned it was Kelly. Mom went to take a bath late that night, and she took the phone with her. She didn't touch the phone, but it lit up on her Facebook page, where her friend's profile appeared. She realized there was her friend with long red hair in a nice short white dress posing. Mom didn't know Kelly with ginger hair."

Simon continued, "When she showed me the picture in the morning, I knew it was her whom I had seen that afternoon, and I was not afraid anymore. But I prayed to her not to show herself to me anymore."

Uma gazed at the boys' faces while discussing spirits and the afterlife. She was deeply concerned about Simon's emotional well-being. She realized the older boy had never mentioned his dance coach's name since he passed. It seemed like he became emotionally paralyzed from his loss. She understood that the death of their beloved coach, whom they considered their grandfather, was shocking. 'One day, you are dancing with him, hugging him, and telling him, 'See you later,' but you never see him again,'; sighed the little one.

'I am so heartbroken for Lara,' said Simon. Lara was Ben's (dance coach) wife. Simon was very close to both. Right after the final farewell, he became quiet and put on weight...a lot. He hated it! His posture became poor, covering his chubby body, and he made degrading comments about himself.

'Look, mom, I have a male breast! I got a C cup. It will be bigger than yours,' he said sarcastically.

Uma was distraught. Simon stopped dancing for a while until Lara gave him a call and said she would like to coach and compete with him again. They started to heal together. They cried and laughed and cried and danced.

Chapter Eight

Guess What Sign?

The weekend was long and tiring. What was supposed to be hours began to feel like days. The boys had multiple lacrosse games on Saturday. Nobody could deny their enthusiasm for the fun coming their way, and they showed it to everyone around. Simon had a dance competition and won multiple categories, but he didn't do as well as prior. Having proven his skills before, something about his victories didn't feel as fulfilling as he had hoped. This was the trouble of keeping expectations too high and falling short. He felt it and was seemingly disappointed about that. The things he expected to perform well or even better at didn't follow the same, and he couldn't get it out of his mind.

Uma tried hard to cheer him up, saying he doesn't need to get a gold medal every single time and to remember bronze is better than rust and silver is better than bronze; you must give yourself more credit and celebrate your achievement.

On the other hand, Matt had a drum recital, and he did it terrifically. Despite feeling a bit nervous at first, he found himself performing brilliantly. His percussion skills flew easily, and as the performance continued, it became more accessible. Once the recital was over, he felt a wave of joy, knowing he had done his part well. Uma went with Simon while Papi attended Matt's recital. Both were quite keen on seeing what was to come. It was nice to take time away from the usual mundane routine and see something new.

After the competitions, they met up in their favorite Korean restaurant. The place was more active and happening than usual. Everyone noticed a familiar face or two. Simon and Matt had quite an appetite and couldn't wait to fill their rumbling tummies.

The competition takes a lot out of a person. All that effort and profuse sweating were bound to make the stomach growl sooner or later. It takes dedication, practice, long hours, and many setbacks that they have to overcome. And so, they were overwhelmed and exhausted from the hard work they had invested in that day. The boys didn't even sit down on their chairs; they practically fell onto them and let out a long sigh. Exhaustion began, and everyone pondered what to eat to ease their hunger. So much work had gone into their competitions; they were relieved it was over.

Uma never called anything a failure. It was the

thinking pattern that did nothing but let a person feel bad more than it should. She had done her fair share of competitions and knew how winning and losing felt. The latter was more important because it taught players how to deal with loss and find the strength to regain. To her, this wasn't defeat. She only talked about setbacks when something did not happen as planned. This time was primarily joyous; they both triumphed on their field.

In the restaurant, they requested to sit inside the air-conditioned room. Even though the competitions were over, they still felt the after-streaking of the heat, having pushed themselves so hard. Uma asked for her margarita and reclined in her seat. She zoned out and enjoyed her spicy drink. Right from the first sip, her tongue felt the rush slowly set in. It panged pretty fast at first and then slowly calmed her down. It was delicious, as always. She tipped her drink to the waiter, who smiled in return. The boys were chatty and silly; they made Papi annoyed! Surprisingly, despite being tired after a long day, they still had enough energy to be annoying. Papi drove a long way. If one thing was guaranteed to tire him, it was the traffic jam. Traffic was on a roll that day, and he had to keep calm as much as he could; too little success. The constant waiting, honking, and turning had helped him feel hungry and angry. He was 'hangry, 'and the serving was slow in the restaurant. They were packed, and there was a lack of employees. This made the wait bothersome, but Papi fought the urge to let this ruin his mood. The boys were already pushing his nerve, so he waited for the best he could. Sooner or later, the food had to come around. He didn't want to ruin everyone's evening, but it certainly wasn't getting any easier. Since the pandemic, so many things have changed. The world had been stuck indoors for months, not weeks. Almost a year was spent staying inside, and people couldn't wait to get outside. Now that the world had opened up again, it took people some time to adapt. The restaurants were still far from catching up to their old pattern of speed and consistency.

Uma told Papi to be patient and grateful for the working people. Too much had happened unexpectedly, and it would take a while before everyone could return to normal. Lucky for them, here they were together now, spending time outdoors.

'I am sure they do as much as they can. They do their best to have our food out as soon as possible. Have a drink. It will take your annoyance away, and we get an Uber home," she giggled.

Papi's expression was ticked off, but something about it came off as more comical rather than serious in

Uma 's eyes.

'Isn't it alcoholism to drink a beer?" asked the younger boy.

'No, silly! There is alcohol in a beer, but alcoholics have a drink or more every day! We don't!"

'But is it healthy? Is it good for your body?"

'Not if it's overdone and abused. Heavy or binge drinking is linked with negative health effects. Drinking regularly and in large quantities can decrease your brain cells and damage your livers."

'Look, our food is coming. Check out the waitress and the busboy. What do you think their zodiac signs are? Simon asked.

The family played an astrology guessing game in each restaurant they ate. They had to check the characteristic of the servers, the way they moved and talked ,and their facial expression.

Uma loved astrology, and she used it in her psychiatric practice. She taught the boys early on to recognize ill characteristics in personality. She believed it could save their life and prevent them from trouble. They studied metacommunication, watched Lie to me, and analyzed the series afterward.

"All right, guys, need to put in your votes -Papi

whispered.

Uma voted for Leo sun sign and Pisces ascendant. She explained that her decision was made on the hair of the girl, which looked like a lion's mane, and she had a sweet, kind, humble personality, and she always helped her co-workers, which is a Pisces trait.

Simon voted Leo ascendant and Sagittarius sun sign. He said the curly, reddish hair belonged to a Leo. Still, her kindness and gentleness, paired with some arrogance while lecturing others, could easily be a Sagittarius trait.

Matt voted for Scorpio because of her piercing. Also, tattoos covered her wrist and arms.

When they finished their meal, they popped the question to Ali, which was the waitress girl's name. They learned a lot about her. They found out she was also studying psychology at the nearby university, and it was her weekend job to support herself financially. Ali would tell them that balancing academics with the job sometimes gets tricky. Yet, both were important to her, and she didn't want to abandon one for the other. The job gave her an income, while the university gave her a set direction on the field she wanted to pursue. Everyone at the table was taken in by her story, and they credited her for her hard work.

She knew her ascendent and moon sign, so Uma

didn't have to erect a chart on her phone. Indeed, she was a Sagittarius ascendant, a Leo sun, and a Scorpio moon. They all guessed correctly, but Simon won the competition this time, and he had the privilege of choosing the next restaurant.

On the ride back home, Uma told them how astrology helped her recognize some mental illness in her patient's charts that was very hard to diagnose otherwise. She truly is look at moon kind of girl.

At home, before they slept, Simon said, "Mommy, you know that was my first competition since Ben died. I thought I couldn't go on the dance floor at one point, but then I felt his arm on my shoulder."

There was a bit of silence at first since this topic was sensitive. However, Uma did not want Simon to feel ignored, so she took a deep breath before asking, 'Do you want to talk about it?"

'No, I don't think so." He replied. 'I just want to know if he is, ok?"

'He is," Uma replied.

'I had a dream with him last night-said, Uma. Ben said we don't know when is our time to go, but when it's a call, we need to. And he had gleaming dance shoes on and was listening to the song of Maneskin, 'I am begging,

begging you. He gave me his bear hug and went into the light. He looked content."

"Ok, I guess," replied the boy.

Simon stared at his trophy for a while and then continued.

"I am sorry, Ben, but my passion for competing died with you. I will keep dancing for fun, but I am done competing."

Uma got shocked, but she didn't want to respond prematurely. Silence. More silence. She didn't know how to respond to all she heard reasonably. The fact that Simon seemed so sure about it bothered her, but she didn't feel it was right to say no. Simon was adamant, and Ben's passing deeply hurt him and everyone. She let herself sit for some time as the silence slowly shifted from discomfort to become more manageable.

Simon kissed his mother and went to sleep. Within seconds his eyes were closed and gone into his dreams. Uma continued sitting there for a while, letting memories rush through her mind. Leaning ahead, she kissed Simon on his cheek and left.

Papi came from having a shower and was disappointed Simon left without kissing him; good night. Uma explained what had just happened. At first, he stood there listening intently and remained quiet. The dream was quite vivid, making Papi wonder for some time. He was about to say something but decided against it. Giving a simple nod, he dried his face with the towel and swung it on his shoulder. It didn't have to be said, but Simon probably needed some company while he slept through the night, so Papi decided to camp on Simon's floor that night. Uma went to sleep with ease. She knew her son had a breakthrough and grieving would be easier from now on. Grieving is a five-stage process - denial, anger, bargaining, depression, and acceptance. The fact that her child was now taking his own steps relieved her.

"At least he talks about death. He talks about him," she sighed out loud to herself.

Weeks went by; some were quick some took an eternity.

One Monday afternoon, both kids came home panicked from school. Uma knew they had heard the news; it was another massive school shooting. They seemed agitated. Having to go to a place where they are promised an education, where they are meant to feel safe. Now here they were, shaking with fear and anger—that excessive fear of being unable to control the situation.

How could any mother help her children when

maniacs were going around? Killing innocents without any remorse. She stood there helpless as the kids stood there with tears and anger in their eyes. Their hands turned into tightened fists that couldn't stop shaking.

'I don't understand. I can't comprehend this ever, mom. This is insane! Why? Why on earth do you hurt children? They were innocent little children! Why did God let this happen? I need you to buy us bulletproof backpacks. I have nightmares of a school shooting, and the red drill triggers me in school."

'I am devastated, truly scattered in pieces. But it's not God, my love. It's the evil, the ill-minded human. There are so many mental illnesses, and it keeps climbing. So much injustice, so much horror. The laws are outdated. It doesn't protect the innocent. It seems like everybody has rights but no responsibilities. It is senseless death, and all could have been prevented. There are always signs before the shooting, clear, loud signs, mostly posted on social media. They post before they strike, but people are numb bystanders. They careless to recognize it and fear to report it."

Uma continued to speak after a pause. 'Ok, kids, let's watch something that will make us forget about this horror. At least, let's try. I know it won't be easy, but thinking about the massacre won't make it any easier. I want you to be at mental peace."

The kiddos loved Adam Sandler's movies and agreed to watch 'Let's go with it 'for the twentieth time. Uma wouldn't necessarily have chosen it, but she went with it. The jokes were silly; Adam was his usual goofy self, while Jennifer Aniston was quirky and lovable as always. The laughs were initially nervous, but slowly and steadily, they began to lose themselves in the movie, and after some time, the hanging tension in the air began to disperse. Uma still struggled to throw herself entirely into the movie's humor, which her child noticed.

"Aren't you in love with this movie? Asked the younger boy. "You seem to be bored."

"I did it the first time, but come on, we have seen it 20x! He is a great, brilliant actor, but he always hires the same team, which makes it dull and always shows his Jewish heritage."

"Oh, my God! Mom, you cannot say that!"

"Yes, I can! I don't insult anyone! My great-grandfather was Jewish. This is the problem. Nowadays, we can't discuss or say anything without hurting somebody's feelings. We all tiptoe around each other and pretend. We describe situations and everything either in emojis or in a long, complicated way, and the essence of the message gets misunderstood or lost. It does not make me an antisemite to acknowledge his stereotypical roles. That's it."

"Isn't this discrimination or racism?" questioned the younger boy. Uma choked up with annoyance.

"No, it's an opinion. It's a choice to like someone or not. When you decide between your strawberry and cotton candy ice cream, don't you prefer one? Or you might like both, but do you always want to eat the same ice cream? Discrimination, racism, and antisemitism come from a superior feeling! When someone thinks that they are more valued and their lives matter more than others. That's wrong, truly deeply wrong. Every single life should be equal on earth."

"Wait a minute! Your great-grandfather was Jewish, so are we also Jewish?"

"Well, Judaism is inherited through the mother, so no. My grandfather, Michael's mother, was an Italian Christian, and they practiced her religion. But you don't need to practice Christianity or Judaism to be decent. All right enough. Now, let's go with it!"

After finishing the movie, they made some easy dinner and ran with the dog by the shore. It was a peaceful, lovely evening. The ocean seemed endless, the stars started to twinkle, and by the time they finished jogging, the moon was up high, sprinkling its silver ray on the shore. The moonlight was doing wonders that night in terms of scenery as the water began shimmering across the coast. There were still some hints of seagulls cawing in far corners, but activity had dimmed.

Chapter Nine

Santa's Mystery

They were happy to shower without arguing. They knew they didn't have to wake up early for the next 14 days because they had finally had their winter break. Winter was always weird since they lived in tropical weather. It was quite a relief for the kids since they had been looking forward to this for quite some time. The school had been quite nerve-wracking, and time away from it was bound to be necessary and healthy. It gave them time to distress and made things easier.

Since time was on their hands, the kids tossed plans left, right, and center about what they wanted to do and where to go. Their suggestions ranged from possible to downright ridiculous, much to Uma 's humor.

"Mom, let's go to Norway for Christmas. I want to see the Northern lights," suggested Simon.

"All right, if you find something affordable and comfortable, a very clean Airbnb, I will consider it. Check all the travel restrictions. It's crazy lately."

"Of course, 'General,'" giggled the teen boy.

"I don't appreciate you calling me that. I know you

guys refer me to that with Papi."

"No, Hon, you are the queen of the house. We all know that fact," laughed her husband.

They discussed the itinerary and their plan for the upcoming travel at dinner. Matt was excited at first to spend Christmas in a snow-covered town. He had always seen it on TV or in photos, but this would be the first time he got to see it with his own eyes.

"Yippie yeh, momsie, finally we can build a snowman. But wait, what about Santa Claus? Is he going to find us? He won't know where we are, will he?"

"You know what? We will go right after Christmas so we won't miss our annual charity ride for the unprivileged!"

The family of four spent Christmas Eve in a Jewish chapel, giving dinner, toys, and clothes to 200 unprivileged families. That became their tradition, and it felt uplifting to give. Uma was often shaking her head on Christmas Eve, mumbling to herself, asking why can't Churches do the same. She thought that instead of going to Christmas mass, why can't more churches follow the tradition of chapels? Giving is an absolute miracle.

To her being charitable did more than go around buying things under the influence of consumerism, which most people were more obsessed with. It felt selfish and unfair. Uma didn't want her boys to take their things for granted, and she made sure they understood the importance of caring for others, regardless of whether they were family, friends, or even strangers.

The boys were intimidated for the first time when Uma signed their family for this Christmas charity. They saw families lacking simple things like chairs and tables. Some were sleeping on the floor, breastfeeding their children on a piece of a deflated air mattress. They didn't have Christmas trees or food to eat.

After Matt learned they would spend Christmas at home, he was relieved.

"Yeees!!! Santa will find me!" he ran off excitedly to play in the garden.

"You will need to tell him the truth. What about your radical honesty in parenting?" asked the older boy.

"Hm, I never said Santa is alive when you guys asked. I only explained where Saint Nickolas (Santa Claus) came from and how he started his gifting before Christmas."

"Oh wow! That's right. You were always a walking Wikipedia mom. I remember Aunt Jata ripping the bandage off from the Santa mystery for me."

"Me too, and I was very angry at her. She had no

right, and you were no longer a believer, and it made me sad. I just found your letter from that Christmas when she lifted the curtain off the mystery. Here read it

"Dear Santa- I mean Jesus.

Since I know Santa passed a while ago, I won't write to him, but since I heard you had been resurrected, you must be somewhere. I can't see you so I will write to you. All I want for Christmas is a puppy, but I can feel I won't get one, so I want you to grant me to sleep in my parents ' room until I don't have any more bad dreams. I also want my parents to love each other forever and ever.

A lot of my friends 'parents got divorced, and I see them sad and crying. I see them being scared, and I would never want to spend Christmas without anyone I love. I also wish to have a DNA test; I want to know my origin and family tree. I think I got posh German blood, but my brother must have some Turkish or gypsy.

I also would like to see snow and play in it and the northern lights. I love you.

This is me, Simon Shuster 9 years old boy "—

"Momsie. You kept this?"

Hm…

"Don't be upset. I was on Santa's mystery for a long time already. I have friends who celebrate Hanukkah and Kwanzaa who have never gotten anything from the big fat guy. Don't forget I got a computer and I did my research. Children might be small, but not stupid mom. My friends told me to look up the ten things our parents were lying about. I was already suspicious when the tooth fairy forgot to take my teeth but left money under my pillow or forgot even the money.

You didn't lie, but you answered something unrelated or answered with questions, using the therapist on me. You still do when you don't want to answer or think Matt is not ready for the truth. "–

"I know, I know," Uma replied. "But the magic of Christmas! The magic is living through believing in Santa. It's beautiful! Watching your face in the morning, trying to figure out where Santa entered to leave some gifts for you, was truly the gift to me."

"No momsie, the magic is living through giving! Why are adults playing along for centuries?"

"Because it feels amazing to give. It truly does. You just said it yourself; that's why we are doing the gift ride. By the way, did you know Saint Nickolas was a Pisces? He was born 15th of March, 270. He was a Greek bishop who also has been known as Nickolas the wonderworker. Besides, he was the secret gift giver; he also did miracles associated with his name. He resurrected three children who were murdered and saved three young girls from prostitution. (Prostitution is when someone engaging sexual activity for some payment.)"

"Prostitution? Back then? Centuries ago?"

"Yes darling, in Saint Nickolas ages. I guess, when he died, they wanted to continue what he created with his secret giving, so people with compassion kept doing what he started, which just spread like fire on the earth and became a tradition. Do you understand? One person made an amazing impact on this world that had survived centuries. Timeless. That is what we need to consider with our actions, our knowledge, and our talents. Add value to humanity. Not like those brainless, valueless Tik Tok videos."

They were getting closer to their gift ride and Christmas Eve dinner. This year they have been invited to their friends. Right after Christmas, the plane took off for Norway. They all have been so thrilled to see the Aurora borealis, the northern lights. That was Uma 's bucket list. A bucket list is a list of adventures the person hopes to achieve during her/his lifetime.

They had already checked so many off their list, Antilope Canyon, the Grand Canyon, the pink and green sand beach of Hawaii, the colored pebbles of lake McDonalds, Uluru in Australia, New Zealand, Iceland glaciers, Niagara Falls, Angel's landing, and so many more. Traveling was their oxygen; their passport was always up to date.

"You know what is the northern light kids?" -started the conversation with Papi to make the time fly by quickly.

"Colorful lights on the sky," answered Matt

"Indeed, but it only appears in high altitude regions, resulting from a disturbance in the magnetosphere caused by the solar wind."

Aurora is derived from the Roman Goddess of dawn, Aurora, who traveled east to west to announce the rising sun. Borealis is named after the ancient Greek God of north wind Boreas." continued Simon, who studied Roman and Greek mythology.

"Mom mythology is grotesque. You say the world we live in is cruel and has so many injustices, but remember what you learned about those mythology figures. They were evil, ill-minded fuckers."

"Hey! Watch your language, young man!" Uma

warned him.

"Look who 's talking?" laughed Papi. "Uma, you curse like a sailor!"

"I have to admit I got a potty mouth, but I am not 13 either."

It was a long overnight flight, so after dinner was served, they all fell asleep. Matt earned the right to be the DJ from the airport to their accommodation.

He chose 'Roxane 'by Arizona Zervas and sang it with all his might. (You never know how inappropriate a song is till you hear your young kids singing it.)

After the song ended, Simon turned to his brother and spoke. "Just so you know, your Roxanne was a spoiled brat, a cocaine addict whore."

Matt did not understand the words he was singing, so he flooded his parents with questions. "Mom, what is cocaine, and what is a whore?"

"Early childhood education is so important," sighed Uma. Thanks to her firstborn, she needed to explain to Matt what those words meant. "

"Mom, what is it again? What is whore?

"Oh, my dear, I had mentioned it once; did you forget?"

She was hoping he would let it go, but he wasn't.

"You know when someone has an intimate relationship in exchange for money.? We call it prostitution, and the slur is whore for it."

"What is intimate again?" Matt asked.

"You know when two people are kissing and hugging…"

She couldn't finish because he cut into her sentence excitedly. "Oh yes!" he chimed. "I know and slow dancing and lit a candle…and you can get money for that?"

"Well, it's prosecuted. You can go to jail for it."

"Not if you marry for money, just like the gold diggers. They exchanging sex for money but in a legal relationship, isn't that true, mom?" Simon continued. "Simon! Enough is enough!" It's hard to explain to your brother what prostitution is.

"And cocaine." Simon pointed out.

She pondered for a while, for a tiny second.

"He got the wrong concept." Uma continued explaining to Matt what cocaine was.

"Do you remember Peru?" she asked. "We had a lot of coca leaf tea to prevent altitude sickness. Cocaine is made out of that. Coca-leaf tea is a natural stimulant made by mother earth. Cocaine is extracted from those leaves through a lengthy chemical process

It is an illegal stimulant drug with so many side effects. It leads to a lot of criminal activities, death, jail."

'How come the leaf is good, but the powder is not?" he asked?"

"Anything highly processed can be deadly for your body, even food. Sugar has addictive tendencies as well.

'Oh, is this the one our Armenian neighbor smokes, the Tijuana?"

They all started to laugh; they were tearing up.

All right, it's time to talk about that, she thought.

"No darling, it's not, and it's not Tijuana. It's marijuana! The queen of the green! It is a healing herb that was forbidden to be used and criminalized. Your body produces cannabinoids in natural homeostasis. Marijuana has a high amount of this chemical."

Uma turned on Damien Marley's medication song. "Listen to this, boys," she said. "Your green leaves, purples, and blue have cured little girl and old women too. I made some great oil for granny Grace when she had breast cancer. My potion is sticky and green, and I named it the Queen of the Green! Thank God it's legalized in many states to help with Alzheimer's, tremors, seizure, cancer."

Uma was an advocate of licensed medical Marijuana. She could prescribe for her patients for anxiety, tremors, some panic attack, insomnia, and grief.

"So can I use Marijuana?" her son asked.

"Absolutely not! You are way too young, and it can make you apathetic, less ambitious, or unmotivated."

"You said it can heal the ill, weren't you?"

"Would you take a headache pill if you do not have a headache? No, you wouldn't, would you? Also, it has healing properties but doesn't heal every single people. Just like medicine, certain medicine suits certain people.

Consumption of marijuana could interfere with a kids' brain development. Unless a child has some major medical illness, should not be used."

"What about heroin and meth and ecstasy?" asked Simon?

"They're all synthetic. They all screw up our minds. It creates addiction after one or two uses. Some are tranquilizing; some give them temporary energy or highs to feel good about themselves for a tiny, tiny short period. It's like you get up to a high mountain with a helicopter without climbing, but two minutes later, you slip and fall, rolling down to the ditch and bumping into stones and dead branches while falling. Then you get the helicopter again to get up to the top of the mountain and fall again, but your body is bruised deeper every time you fall. Simple as it is. Drugs are making people want to escape reality. It always has the worst impact on our bodies. There are also prescription drugs and alcohol. People who suffer from addiction are not fulfilled. They most likely are unhappy or unaccomplished and need to self-medicate and numb themselves because reality hurts.

"Matt is addicted to Fortnight; you must limit that for him."

"I agree; that's why I make him busy with sports and

traveling. However, children need boredom to use their imagination. It's not ok to overschedule them because, as an adult, they won't be able to manage their life if there is nothing to do. I am addicted to caffeine; without it, I feel angry and get headaches. The only time I didn't drink coffee while pregnant and breastfeeding, you guys. But you both must understand it's tough to get healed from addiction, and it's better never to try it."

"I definitely won't." her son said. I remember visiting the addictology with you when the babysitter canceled, and you had to take us to work. When we crossed in front of the hospital rooms, we saw some people coming off drugs and alcohol. They were in pain, they looked awful, and it was imprinted in my brain. You mentioned something like Delir terman."

"Delirium Tremens," Uma corrected him. "I am sorry you had to see it, but the positive side is that you most likely won't have a poor decision in this matter. You will make so many mistakes in life, but this is very hard to correct. I work with addicts. It is tearing so many families apart. Ruining lives, and most of the time ending very badly."

"Isn't your brother an addict?" Simon asked.

"Yes, Simon, he is, but Connor has a gambling

addiction. It 's not better. Addiction is connected with low serotonin levels in our brains. It needs to be stimulated; some find the wrong way and substance to activate it. Connor got stimulation from gambling. Now he does not gamble anymore but hunting. He just traded one addiction for another, like many seeking enlightenments from Ayahuasca.

They call it medicine, and it can be perilous. Some seek enlightenment from this hallucinogen that could heal mental illnesses under professional supervision. However, many drug addicts making a trade changed their substance using Ayahuasca and hallucinogen mushrooms instead. Mushrooms, also can be used in micro-dose amounts to treat depression with the help of medical professionals."

The car suddenly hydroplaned on the snow, but Papi saved it, thanks to God his excellent driving experience. They all got intimidated, so they stopped talking and looked through the window in silence, watching the natural wonders of Norway.

Hours later, they arrived at their base. It was a heated glass igloo they rented. Very unique, and they had animal fur blankets to protect them from the arctic winter. It was snowing all day; fluffy soft snow covered the entire land close and far. The evening sky was covered with stars; no unwanted, excessive light pollution disturbed this perfection.

They were excited for the next day. They signed up for a tour where they could see polar bears and arctic animals in a distance.

That night a miracle happened. A solar storm was coming, and they finally saw the northern lights. They could see the purple, green, and blue lights dancing high in the sky, putting up the most incredible show you can imagine. And all from their glass igloo while sitting on their bed.

It was brilliant, showed dynamic patterns, and appeared as curtain rays, spirals, and flickers that covered the entire sky.

"This is my serotonin stimulation, mom." sighed the teen.

Another ah-ha moment, another unbelievable experience.

Chapter Ten

Home Sweet Home

They had a great week in Norway, and they were pleased with the Norwegian people's hospitality and found the nation very intellectual. They spent New year's Eve in Norway with the families whom they met during their trip. They made a wishing board on their computer and went to bed after midnight.

They had a tradition to rise on the first day of the year with the rising sun and visualize their year ahead. A week later, they were ready to go back from the arctic cold to their tropical paradise.

"Home sweet home," Papi said. "I love to travel, but I miss my bed every time. I guess I am getting older."

"Talk for yourself," said his wife. "However, I agree I love our bed and always great to see our fur baby. You guys need to get ready, in a few days school will start again."

"Stop, Mom, I can't think of school yet!" yelled the younger boy.

Uma's phone started to ring, but as usual, she had to run around to find it. It was her brother from Australia, Connor. Uma's brother called to announce that his wife was pregnant but needed an abortion because she had cervical cancer. They had three children already and a higher chance of survival if she terminated her pregnancy.

Uma was heartbroken for his brother and wife but was there for them to listen. Later, when she finished the phone call, she told Papi about the sad news. The boys were ear-dropping, of course. Simon had some valid questions.

"Mom," Simon asked, "I am confused about abortion. The fetus has a heartbeat at 4,5,6 weeks after conception. When you terminate a pregnancy, you decide to end a life.

"Indeed," she replied. "You also have to know that every single case is unique. All women should have reproductive rights. I had an ectopic pregnancy, it wasn't a vial pregnancy, so if nature had taken care of it, I would have died. I felt the symptoms and could go before it ruptured, so I was sick but did not die. Auntie has cancer; her survival rate might be higher if she gets the treatment she chooses. She has chosen chemotherapy.

"Chemotherapy? Her son asked. "Didn't you say it ruins the person's system,"

"That's right." she nodded. "But this is also supposed to be a choice of the individual. In many cases, it can help. Just like a snake bite can be treated with the same poison.

When Grandma Grace had cancer, she went with holistic treatment and went in remission with medical marijuana and essiac tea, but every soul should be able to decide for themself."

"So, are you pro-choice?"

"Well, this is a tricky question to answer. I believe in individuals' right to make their decisions. However, I also think if a woman has more than two abortions, they are most likely irresponsible in not using protection. It could be a debating case, especially in countries where everything is given to prevent unwanted pregnancies.

However, as I told you, it's not that simple. We, the women, all have our individual stories. Some women get raped. Why should they keep a pregnancy from abuse? How is it possible to love an offspring from an act of violence? Incest? Some get violated by their father, brother, or grandfather. Some women are capable of loving a child from sexual abuse.

There was a story about an abducted teen, captured for years in a den, and got impregnated. She had her baby, and her son was seven years old when she escaped. She wouldn't give him up for anything. I read a sad book, 'Somaly Mam, the lost innocence. It's about sex-trafficked children in Asia, mainly in Vietnam, the Philippines, and

India. They are sold for sex slavery at a very early age. Boys and girls. They have no reproductive rights. That book was so heavy on the soul that I purged while reading. That 's why I can 't watch Superball because the highest sex trafficking going on during Superball.

Privileged, wealthy, mature, ill-minded monsters buy unprivileged children for their ill pleasure. I hate them with passion!"

Uma got so aggravated talking about the book started to curse and cry. Papi had to stop her.

"Enough, jeez!" he snapped. "This is horror! He only asked about abortion!"

Uma took some deep breaths and changed the narrative.

"One of my great aunts had an unsuccessful abortion 46 years ago." Uma continued. "She had to be around three months far in her pregnancy. Six months later, she gave birth to a healthy boy, who cared for her last while dying from Alzheimer 's. He was a miracle, a true blessing in her life. We don 't know how this could happen, but it did.

Others got an opportunity to be adopted and live a beautiful, valuable, meaningful life because their birth parents considered keeping and giving them up for adoption. They made another couple happy who were not able to conceive. But there are also cases when doctors detect genetic diseases in the fetus that will shorten the baby 's life or make it painful and very limited. So, do you hear what I say?

There is no right and wrong; all cases are different. We cannot judge anybody 's situation until we walk a mile in their shoe.

But yes, women should always have the right to make a decision. This is our reproductive rights."

"I agree," said Papi. 'However, fathers always should be involved with the decision."

'Perhaps not all the time," Uma pointed out. "An abuser should never have the right to decide those cases."

The family spent the last two days of winter break with their friends on the beach. They loved pedal boarding and surfing. They were blessed with excellent friends. Compassionate, honest friends with similar values. People who cared a lot for nature, animals, and other humans.

Some of their friends adopted children into their families; some adopted animals, some helped out in homeless shelters, and some traveled with them through the nonprofit. 'There for You 'was an organization Papi founded. This was a non-profit organization that the Shuster family founded to make a difference. It took them places, most of the time in second and third-world countries, where human compassion and help were desperately needed.

They visited Bali, Costa Rica, Thailand, Peru, Jamaica, and Ecuador through 'There for You. 'They spent two weeks everywhere they went. For one week, they volunteered in orphanages or schools, teaching English, and the second week they were taken by a native guide to visit places and natural wonders of the country where they stayed.

The meals and housing were provided and traded for their help. Uma believed this was the best way to teach her sons to care for others. And they did. They did! They cared a lot! A few of their SOUL FAMILIES, that 's how Uma referred to their friends, had special needs children. Some had autism, some were born with genetic diseases, and one was paralyzed from an accident.

In the beginning, the boys were unsure how to handle a child with special needs but quickly learned to show love and be there for their friends and siblings.

They often had been asked to take care of peers with special needs on school trips and been asked to go to birthdays and support children who had no friends. At one point, it became overwhelming. Uma never realized she asked too much from her kids.

Chapter Eleven

Talking To the Moon

When Simon became a teen, he was invited to parties and activities with children with no similar interests. He felt guilty about declining, but one day he exploded. It happened on the last day of winter break.

Two of the 'loner kids' moms texted him and invited him to the movies. He had no intention of going. He had plans to go pedal boarding with his friends. Uma told him it's nice to support the ones who can't fit in anywhere. That's when he started to break down.

"Do you see what you are doing?" he shouted. "You are making me feel guilty, mom. I can't stand this!"

"What do you mean?" Uma asked, taken aback. "You were there for them forever!

"Yes, because I feel bad; I feel guilty about how lucky I am. You made me do it. I want to help mom; I want to! But I want to be with my friends, the kids I choose. Kids I can laugh with and talk about girls with.

Why should I spend the last day of my break with someone who does not even talk to me or can't behave? Jeez! Do you remember when you made us go to the restaurant with one of your boxing friends and her kids? They were embarrassing! You felt sorry for the woman after her husband cheated on her. Those kids behaved like animals. She climbed on the dinner table, and they were throwing food. And the mother ignored them. And what did you do? You were trying to redirect children you have nothing to do with. It 's crazy! That 's not your place. Not your karma. Aren 't you the one who says not my monkey, not my zoo? Live it. I don 't feel responsible for the entire world."

Papi came from the garage quickly to the rescue. He was concerned, having heard them arguing. Since Simon became a teenager, the boy often argued with Uma.

"That 's enough, you two!" he shouted. "Simon, you have no right to yell at mommy. And you, Uma! This is enough! The boys are kind, polite, and compassionate. You can 't force them to be there for everyone. Remember what your grandma Vanda said. She said you couldn't save the whole world. Make sure you and your family are happy first, and try to make a small daily impact. It doesn 't mean you need to give your precious time to everyone and take the joy away from yourself. Don 't be a people pleaser.

A smile, a kind compliment, helping an elderly cross the road, buying a book for kids who can 't afford it. You must understand that kind and friendly doesn't mean everyone belongs at your dinner table."

Uma was shocked. She was a Pisces sun, very compassionate, and always serving others. She didn't know how to claim boundaries. She was seemingly disturbed by that fact; her blindfold might have hurt her children, requiring so much understanding and being a source of comfort to others. She started to remember Vanda's words.

"You only need to learn three sentences. Thank you, I am sorry, and NO!!! NO is liberating! NO is respect! NO is uplifting!"

She made herself a cup of tea and retreated to her favorite place. The patio looked over the ocean. It was a waxing gibbous moon. Sitting silently, she realized she didn't even make a new year's resolution. She looked up at the moon and imagined Vanda and her husband, Uma's favorite grandpa, Michael, sitting hand in hand and listening to the gypsies playing the violin. At least that's what grandpa Michael told her when she was a little girl.

He was the best storyteller. He said that when he dies, he will sit on the moon and listen to the gypsies who play violin on the moon. He said he would listen to her if she ever needed to talk; she could speak to the moon.

She could hear them laughing and repeatedly saying,

'you left out the joy; you left it out. Remember, you can't give water from an empty well."

When she fell back to reality, Uma grasped a piece of paper and started to write a note to herself to remember what was important from now on.

'Don't take it personally because it isn't, 'she wrote. 'I will do it out of love and respect. Self-love and self-respect. This is my new year, new me resolution. '

She won't fool herself this time by promising to lose weight, eat less chocolate, and exercise more. She had it hard for a while. She lost so many friends last three years. Some died, and some disappeared on her. She was still crippled by that unbearable pain when she thought about them. She never bothered anyone with her grief; she wanted to protect them. She battled with her darkest agony on her own. She wanted to be rescued but never asked for it, so she became her own superhero. Staying awake night after night analyzing. Often, she felt she couldn't breathe anymore! Broken into pieces! It was hard to scoop herself up from time to time. However, she did! She did it for her boys and friends. She did it for YOU, maybe!

She misunderstood and thought her life was spared when she was born, only to help others. So, she did it out of compassion. Never expect anything in return, so often she had been used. She is the one you could lean on, gave her shoulders to cry on. You find comfort in her wisdom and knowledge, her voice is peaceful, and her advice is soulful. It's easy to feel close to her; she is Peace. You find her where people are in need. Homeless shelters, orphanages, hospitals! She is like Santa Claus; she is the book- fairy lady. She has an excellent ear for listening, and she keeps it for herself. Secrets! All the secrets that she cannot tell anyone consume her slowly.

Some misunderstood her compassion and fell in love with her. Both men and women. Some took her kindness for granted and squeezed her till she felt suffocated, till there was nothing more to give or say. She has never been greedy and always chose integrity and intellect, so she often became a project for some bored privileged. She knows it's wrong.

Remember, friendship cannot be a one-way street because they often end up at dead ends. It always gives and takes. She realizes she doesn't want to be a rubbish bin or an umbrella that shelters all from the storm but is forgotten when the sun is shining.

Finally, she remembered. So, she had changed, just like that. At the moment, she chose joy, laughter, peace, and dancing in the rain. She turned the page. Just like that. and started over on a beautiful white paper waiting to be filled with happy memories.

Thank You!

About the Author

Uma Kriko is a pen name. Krisztina has chosen this name because of her second-born son, who couldn't talk till he turned 3.5 years old.

His only word was Uma, and he referred to the full moon. Watching the full moon rise is her family's favorite monthly event.

Kriko is the name her favorite grandpa called her when she was a little girl. It's genuinely sentimental.

Uma is a Hungarian-American author and mother of two teen boys.

She had her education as a special education teacher, drama therapist, and psychiatric nurse.

She is obsessed with astrology and herbalism.